The Thief & His Hunter

Book 1

BY

Eidahs

COVER & EDITING BY
BINKY INK

BINKY INK

THE LITERARY ARM OF BINKY PRODUCTIONS

WWW.BINKYPRODUCTIONS.COM/THETHIEFANDHISHUNTER

Table of Contents

CHAPTER 1

Conor took the photograph of the tiara from the siblings, studying it carefully. His hood covered most of his face, casting a shadow over most of his features, so he was careful when he looked up again to politely meet his clients' gazes without revealing *too* much of his face.

'Do you think you can retrieve it for us?' asked the young woman.

Conor nodded. 'This was stolen recently, yes? I think I can track it down easily.'

'That tiara was our grandmother's,' the brother offered. 'My sister has always been intent on wearing it to Prom.'

'When did it go missing?' asked Conor, placing the photo back on the table.

'Just last week. After the break-in.'

Conor thought about that. Most items he stole back for clients had been claimed long ago and sat in mansions or museums. This tiara either sat in a pawn-shop or in someone's home. Conor was no detective, but he had his ways of sniffing out anyone who was sus.

'I'll find it,' he assured.

'We filed a report with the Investigative Department of Police, but they wouldn't tell us what they found about any suspects.'

'Then I'll just have to break into the station.'

The brother gave Conor his payment – he always took half up-front. The young woman smiled at him.

'Maybe once you've found it, I can thank you properly.' She tucked a strand of hair behind her ear.

Conor chuckled, flattered. 'Sorry, but I'm gay. Not to mention far too old for you.' He reckoned he was at least a decade older.

Her brother stifled a laugh, nudging his sister.

Conor walked back to the window, glancing out. 'You never saw my face,' he declared, lifting his leg over the open window's railing.

'Hey, Vulpis?'

Conor paused and looked back at the siblings.

'Why did you choose that name for yourself?'

Conor grinned. 'Because I'm the sly fox.' He winked before leaping out of the window. He rolled to cushion his fall a storey and a half below.

He ran to the nearest apartment complex and scaled its fire escape stairs to the roof. He ran across the roof and leapt over the gap between the two blocks, the Autumn wind on his face, time almost stopping as the rush of the escape thrilled him. He landed in another roll. Then jumped down to a penthouse balcony, grabbed the railing, and swung out to the next roof, one storey lower. And off Conor bounded from roof to roof to his destination.

* * *

'What do you mean we got broken into? We're an investigative branch for the police, we've got security cameras all around the building. No one breaks into this place.' Theron slapped a hand to his forehead.

Martha stared back, looking amused. 'That's why I called you. Because the cameras caught a glimpse of our culprit.'

Sighing, Theron waved for his boss to go on and show him. She played the security footage on their high-tech screen. It showed a man leaping down the building from two stories higher. He was clad in black leather attire and wearing the signature hood of the very thief Theron had been hunting for years.

'Vulpis.' Theron paused the recording. 'That's why he got in undetected. Because he came during a time when few of us were here.' He pointed at the screen. 'No chance he turned around so we could see his face?'

'Vulpis is good. Never looks directly at the security cams.' Martha pointed at a corner of the screen. 'He used a slingshot to take out the adjacent camera.'

'A slingshot?' Theron shook his head in disbelief. 'I haven't heard of anyone using those since I was a kid.' He chuckled. 'Used to practise with my best friend all the time.'

'The one who got away?' asked Martha.

'Yeah. The one who moved away.' Theron strode out of the room. 'So what's our next step? How do we catch Vulpis? Feels like forever since I took over from

Barry.' He shrugged. 'I'm never going to catch him at this rate.'

Martha followed as Theron grabbed his jacket and began towards the exit.

'There have to be witnesses to his crimes,' Theron went on. 'People who've seen his face.'

'No one talks. They all claim he helped them retrieve stolen goods.'

'Stolen goods?' Theron stopped, turning around. '*Vulpis* steals them. He breaks into museums, rich people's homes. He's breaking the law and getting on my nerves the longer I hunt him down to no avail.' Theron started off again. 'I can't wait to get my hands on him.'

* * *

Conor studied the layout of the house he was to steal from. The police report mentioned an identified suspect based on fingerprints. The burglar had taken the tiara to a pawnshop, as suspected. However, someone had already purchased the tiara and the shop owner ensured confidentiality of his clients.

The mansion had security cameras and guards patrolling the lavish gardens. Either this person was a successful businessperson or part of a mafia. Mobsters were easier to negotiate with if anything went wrong. Conor usually could offer to retrieve something for them and that sufficed. Anyone else, however, anyone who followed the law diligently, no negotiations possible.

Conor crept closer, keeping his hooded head below the bushes. He'd have to find a way around the guards. He wasn't trained to take them out. He was trained to scale, run, jump, and steal.

Finally, he saw his opening. He ran in a half-crouch across the terrain and jumped like a ballerina over the sprinklers, avoiding them. He pressed his back to the wall just as a guard rounded the corner. He turn-rolled, pressing himself to the bricks and slunk along to the large patio doors.

Lockpicking his way in, Conor tentatively slid the door open. So far so good. Aiming his slingshot, he sent a rock at the security camera in the corner of the room. It turned away from the door. Now Conor could creep along past here without being seen.

Grinning to himself, Conor left the patio door ajar before working his way to the side of the house. He jumped, latching onto a windowsill and pulled himself up. When he stood on the windowsill, he grabbed onto some of the jutting bricks and scaled his way to the roof.

He crept along the roof to an empty room's window. Grabbing the gutter, he dangled himself, slid his little stainless steel card-knife glass cutter along the side of the glass and sliced the window open with practised ease. He lowered himself just enough, angling his legs, and slunk into the dark room.

* * *

Martha marched to Theron. 'We've got a lead. Someone's tipped us off about a man, perhaps thirties, asking about a stolen tiara from a pawnshop owner. Matches the reports. We think he might be headed for whoever purchased this tiara.'

'Then it's time to crash the party.' Theron secured his gun, feeling a thrill. This was the first time in a long time they had a viable lead on Vulpis.

'Be careful,' Martha warned. 'We don't want to harm this guy. We want to take him in and question him. People praise him. And those of us hunting him . . .'

'Yeah, yeah, they're calling me the detective who's hounding him.' Theron became defensive. 'I never even met the guy. How am I supposed to be hounding a lawbreaker? A lawbreaker!'

'Just remember we want him alive.'

'Oh, I remember. I've been after this thief for so long, I *want* him alive, if only so he can answer all my questions.'

Theron gathered a small team and they left stealthily for the mansion where Vulpis was said to be.

* * *

Conor had the tiara. He wrapped it in a small shawl and stuffed it in his satchel. He was ready to make his way to his exit, and if he couldn't, he had that Plan B he'd secured earlier. There'd been no alarms. So far everything was going smoothly.

Conor paused. The corridor was quiet, but he heard something downstairs. A fast pitter-patter of shoes.

Conor cursed under his breath. The police were here – only *they* were this stealthy.

Conor veered the corner and entered the room he'd come in from. He peered out the window and saw officers sneaking along the perimeter. He couldn't exit from there.

Conor turned back and hurried to another room. It was an office of sorts – it would have to do. He ran to the window, peering out carefully.

Good, it seemed the officers were focused on his backup exit – that left this side of the house unguarded.

Conor lifted the window open, ready to jump out, when—

'Vulpis! Hands above your head.'

Conor paused as he heard the click of a gun. He stuck his head out the window. There was no easy access to the roof from here, nor to the ground, but there was a ladder just leaning against the wall – below it, paint cans. Conor couldn't believe his luck. He chuckled.

'I said hands above your head, thief.'

Aware of the gun aimed at his back, Conor slowly brought his hands up, preparing himself. If he could just bring the ladder closer. He reached an arm out, pulling on it. It teetered towards the window but got stuck on a jutting brick, still too far to help Conor down. *These fancy people and their fancy bricks.* These had served him moments before – not now.

The rush of footsteps alerted Conor to the officer squarely behind him – it was too late. The man pulled on Conor's hood, spinning him around to point his gun in his face.

Conor stared wide-eyed at the man who apprehended him. Taller than he remembered him, dark hair covering his thick brows, a thin goatee neatly trimmed around his luscious lips, his dark blue eyes vivid in contrast to the dim light that seemed to give his pastel skin a soft glow. And he was so much more handsome, it staggered Conor's heart.

'Theron?'

* * *

Theron gaped at the blond man before him, pale blue eyes just as earnest as he remembered them. He had a subtle hint of facial hair, far less pronounced than Theron's own, but enough to mark his years, and it made him all the more gorgeous.

'Conor?' Theron worked his jaw. 'You're . . . *you're* Vulpis?' Theron took a staggering step back. 'You're the thief I'm after?'

Conor grinned. 'So you're my hunter?'

Theron raked a hand through his hair, lowering his gun hand. He couldn't believe it. 'Damn, it's been . . . fifteen years.' He pressed his lips together. 'Fifteen years since you left.'

'Since *I* left?' Conor was defensive. 'I had no choice. My parents were moving – I *had* to follow them.'

'Across the country, several states away?'

'What was I supposed to do?' shrugged Conor. 'We were fifteen. Besides, it's not like my best friend was going to stop me because he decided to hate me.'

'I was angry, okay? You were abandoning me!'

Conor palm-clapped as he emphasised. 'I didn't abandon you. I had no choice but to follow my parents when we moved away.' He deflated. 'A mistake I learnt a year later when I . . .' He sighed.

Something clanked outside.

'Look, I *thought* you were abandoning me, okay?' Theron motioned towards the outside. 'You were leaving, so I decided to break up with my best friend because that was easier than dealing with abandonment.'

Conor's eyes reflected sadness, and it tugged at Theron's heart. 'I hadn't realised you felt that way.'

'Yeah, well.' Theron shrugged. 'Not that it matters now anyway.' He snapped himself back. 'We're grown-ups, and you're an infamous thief. I have been hunting you for many years. Now I get to identify who Vulpis is and track you down wherever you go.' Theron let out a soft chuckle. 'I guess apprehending you has turned into a catch-up.'

Conor grinned cheekily. 'Only if you can keep up and catch me.'

Conor leapt out of the window.

'Conor!'

Theron closed the distance to the window, reaching his arm out to grab Conor. And missing him. When he looked out, he couldn't see Conor, nor tell where or if he had landed safely.

Theron cursed under his breath. That taunt was exactly what Conor had told him the first time they'd met, when they were five. And Theron had caught him then – he would catch him now.

Theron ran back the way he'd come and down the stairs. He rushed out of the mansion, and saw movement in his periphery. He sprinted towards Conor who leapt over a short fence. Theron easily jumped over it, quickly catching up with the thief.

Conor reached the emergency stairs for an apartment building. Theron followed him up to the roof where Conor ran and jumped over the gap to the next roof.

Theron stopped on the edge of the roof, looking down, his heart pounding.

'You can do it.'

Theron was startled, realising Conor was staring at him from across the gap, arms crossed, a grin on the side of his mouth.

Theron motioned between them. 'What is this? You some sort of parkour expert now or something?'

'Actually, yes.' Conor approached the gap. 'Give yourself a running start, then leap like a ballerina when you jump.' Theron furrowed his brows, puzzled. 'Don't worry, Theron. I'll catch you. I won't let you fall.'

Theron merely gaped at him. Despite the situation, it was like no time had passed at all, almost like they had seen each other yesterday and were picking up where they had left off.

'You want to catch me, right? You want to have that catch-up?'

Theron pointed behind him. 'At the station!' Conor merely waited. 'You haven't changed one bit. You're just as reckless.' Theron rolled his eyes, clipping his gun to his belt. 'If I fall and break a limb . . .'

Conor reached a hand out towards him. 'I'll make sure you're safe.'

Theron felt crazy for considering this. He dreaded being high up, let alone on a roof like this. 'Fine.'

He backed away, took a deep breath, and then ran, leaping over the gap between the two buildings. Time stopped as the cool air whipped past his face.

His foot landed on the edge of the next rooftop. Conor grabbed Theron's hand, pulling him to him, and wrapped an arm around his waist, pressing him close to his body.

'I've got you.'

Theron had to look away, his head already feeling hot, aware that his face was nearly touching Conor's. Yet, the way the moon shone on Conor's face, emphasising the flush on his usually ivory cheeks, had Theron wanting to stare at him all night. It seemed like time had stopped, and a rush of heat threatened to make Theron forget himself.

Conor took a step back, leading Theron to the safety of the wide rooftop.

Theron stopped. He had so many questions. 'You could have tried to keep in touch,' he blurted.

Conor raised his brows. '*You* broke up with *me!* A harsh friendship break-up. I thought you hated me! It devastated me. It wasn't up to *me* to reach out to *you* after that. I was hurt.'

'Yeah, well, I was hurt too.'

Conor spread out his arms. 'Why didn't you just tell me that instead of acting like you hated me?'

'I don't know. It was easier, I guess. I thought you *wanted* to move away. I thought you wanted to leave me behind.'

'I was heartbroken about the move,' admitted Conor. 'Didn't know you felt just as heartbroken.'

'Yeah well, that's because . . .' Theron paused. His heart was beating so fast.

Theron and Conor stared at each other.

'I cried myself to sleep,' admitted Theron. It had wrenched his heart.

'Same.'

Then they spoke at the same time.

'Because I was in love with you.'

'Because I loved you.'

Eyes wide, both men dropped their jaws.

'You're gay too?' asked Conor, his surprise turning into a soft grin.

'Bi, actually,' said Theron. His breath hitched and he exhaled shakily. He averted his gaze.

Small hints of colour appeared on the horizon as the sun began to rise. Theron saw Conor's shadow approach as the thief took a step forward. He touched Theron's chin with his fingers, tilting it up slowly. Theron's heart skipped a beat.

Conor cupped Theron's face. 'And now? How do you feel seeing me after all these years? Because I can tell you right now, it doesn't matter how long it's been. I never stopped feeling things for you. And seeing you now is making me feel a lot more than I ever have before.'

Theron was trembling. He was nervous, and he was excited. 'It doesn't matter how I feel about you, Conor. We were teenagers. Maybe it might have worked out then, had we known, had we been able to admit it to each other. But I'm a detective, you're a thief.'

'I help people,' Conor insisted gently.

'You break the law.'

'*You* haven't changed one bit. Always such a stickler for rules.' Conor's tone was tender.

Theron downcast his eyes. 'We can't be together. How would it work?'

'I wasn't asking about the logistics of it. I was asking how you feel.'

Theron met Conor's gaze. 'Seeing you again . . . It's brought it all back. I knew it was you right away, as soon as I saw your face, and my heart leapt. It soared, and sank.' He paused. Conor waited. 'I still have feelings for you too. I think I always have, like you, continued to care even while pretending I had moved on with my life.'

Conor's smile was tender and it sent warmth to Theron's heart.

'Then we can figure this out, no? Now that we know how we feel about each other and how we felt back then too.'

Theron shook his head, and Conor removed his hand from Theron's face, his brows creasing with disappointment.

'I'm sorry. But I have to take you in, Conor.'

In one swift motion, Theron unclipped his gun and brought it up, holding it with both hands. 'Hands above your head, Vulpis. I need to take you in for questioning.'

Conor chuckled, backing away from Theron. Theron set his jaw. 'Conor, don't make this more difficult than it needs to be, *please.*'

'We'll talk again soon, I hope. We have a lot to unpack and resolve, it seems.' His smile turned into a grin. 'But you're worth it. Somehow, now that I know what that break-up was about, it says a lot about us. And meeting again . . .?'

'Conor?' Theron warned.

Conor merely grinned at him and winked. Then he fell back, hands grabbing onto the edge of the roof.

'Conor!' Theron screamed. He ran to him, peering down and barely catching sight of Conor slipping into an open window below.

Theron backed away from the edge of the roof, clutching his chest as he realised he feared more for Conor's safety than he was worried about catching him.

Breathing heavily, Theron waited to steady himself before making his way down.

<u>Chapter 2</u>

'I thought you apprehended him!' chided Martha.

'I thought so too.'

'And you didn't see his face?'

'He's got that hood that hides his face.' Theron continued past Martha. He had to process the shock of seeing Conor again.

Entering his office, Theron slammed the door. He leaned his back on it.

Anyone else would think he was pissed about his failure. In reality, he was reeling. Somehow he knew he had never stopped loving Conor. He always thought about him. His hyperfocus on catching Vulpis had kept his mind off him. And now – *Vulpis was Conor!*

Theron chuckled to himself . . . and *at* himself.

He'd never dared tell Conor how he felt about him. He wasn't entirely sure he knew back then how much in love he was. And Conor loved him too?

'He declared his love to me,' Theron murmured to himself, awed. He could hardly believe it. Subconsciously, Theron had been chasing Conor, chasing this feeling of loving in this way, ever since.

Theron pushed away from the door and walked over to his desk. He looked Conor up online, searching for his social media profiles. He wasn't finding much. If Conor lived in the city, it was under a different name, Theron realised.

When they were kids, they would take on different names or make prank calls as relatives. Theron tried all the names he could remember.

'Vulpis,' he whispered. 'You sly fox. Didn't make this easy on me, did you?'

Theron folded his arms on his desk and buried his face in them.

* * *

Conor was walking on cloud nine, relishing in Theron's touch, even if it had been brief. It felt just as elating as if they had kissed. Theron was so much more handsome now, with that dark bit of facial hair, a goatee so well trimmed, short and subtle, contouring his lips and making them look so kissable, tempting Conor every time he looked at them.

'He loved me, that's why. It explains so much! He was and has been in love with me this whole time!' Conor skipped to his couch and jumped to land lying down on it, hands clasped behind his head. 'I told him I loved him. I finally did it. I finally told the man I've always loved how I feel.' Conor grinned. 'I feel so happy, Fidelis.'

Conor glanced down at the golden retriever. He clapped on his thigh and Fidelis leapt up on top of Conor. He began scratching her head.

'Good girl!' Fidelis barked happily in return. 'Now, if only Theron could let go of his rules. Sure, I break the law, but it's for a good cause.' Amidst his joy, there was also yearning.

Fidelis made a whimper of sympathy before resting her head on Conor's chest. Conor rested a hand on her back.

'What are we going to do about that, eh? Got any ideas?'

Fidelis inclined her head to the side, making another soft sound of sympathy.

'Yeah, thought so.'

Conor closed his eyes, feeling the fatigue overcome him, and replayed his encounter with Theron over again in his mind until he drifted off.

* * *

Theron fidgeted. 'He always leaves.' He muttered to himself. 'Again, he left. He left me. And now I'm left just waiting high and dry.'

He realised he was voicing his frustrations out loud. He sat in the back of the van where he and his team were being driven to the new location a tip claimed was where Vulpis would strike.

'Bad date?' one of the officers asked.

Theron hesitated. 'Something like that.'

She gave Theron a wry smile. 'In my experience, men who make me run after them aren't worth it.'

'Making me run after him.' Theron chuckled. 'You don't know the half of it.'

The van stopped and Theron stood.

'All right. We shoot to warn. Tasers to shock. Capture is our goal. This guy is a lawbreaker but he's not a criminal.'

One of the other detectives, Lorenzo, narrowed his eyes. 'Aren't those the same thing?'

'Not in my book. Yeah, he's thieving, it's a crime, but he's not . . .' Theron rubbed his forehead. He didn't have time to argue about this. 'I just want to catch him. I need Vulpis!'

Theron realised he'd said that more forcefully than he wanted to. He cursed himself and the heat that rose to his cheeks. He cursed the implications of his words and how true they were, in every sense.

When he thought too much about Conor, he could still feel the blond man's arm wrapped around his back, his warm hand cupping his cheek. His lips twitching into a smile. That wink, that grin. Just the same as always, but so much more handsome, so much more enticing, and so much more—

'Sir?'

Theron realised everyone else had stepped out of the van and was waiting for him to take the lead.

Theron jumped out of the back of the van and hurried into the jeweller's shop. It was one of the high-end larger shops that sold all sorts. It was huge. They even had a section on the third floor where they sold antiques. And that was where Vulpis had struck.

The team reached the floor in question. Security systems had been taken out, a bit more crudely than Theron would have expected – the window had been broken into, and shattered glass lined the wall where Vulpis had come through.

'The glass from this vitrine has been sliced by a special glass cutter,' one of the detectives observed.

'How does one cut through glass without making a sound?' asked Theron.

'Must be a special knife or something.'

'Or something.' Theron tilted his head to the side, noticing the lovely pillow in the centre of the display case. 'What was stolen from this? Rings?'

'A brooch.' Lorenzo pointed at the description on the side of the display case.

'A brooch!' Theron scanned the area. The place was quiet and empty, aside from his team. He walked around the area, muttering to himself. 'Where are you hiding, Vulpis?' He looked up at the beams above him, hoping to find Conor perched up there.

'Hey Theron, Vulpis left a calling card.'

Theron looked back and returned to the display case.

'More like, love letter,' the other officer teased. She handed Theron a note that was delicately written on beautiful stationery.

Theron's heart leapt as he took the note and turned it over to study it. He recognised Conor's handwriting. It was his letter handwriting, the one he saved for special occasions.

Swallowing, Theron read in his head. *Had to leave early. I'll be thinking of you.* Beside the words, Conor had drawn a heart.

Theron found himself placing his hand on his chest – as if that would quell his racing heart.

'I'm going to hold onto this.' He sighed. 'We missed him. Vulpis isn't here.' The disappointment was apparent in Theron's voice, and he didn't care how it was perceived.

He took a few steps away from the others, re-reading the note Conor had left him. Theron traced his finger along Conor's delicate handwriting. Vulpis had never left a note behind before. This was the first time. And that was exactly what Martha had noted as soon as the team returned to H.Q.

'What changed?'

'What changed to make him leave this behind?' Theron kept staring down at the note. In his mind, he answered, *I am the reason.* He wanted to believe it was because Conor had come face to face with him, that that was what had changed.

Theron did *not* want to let go of this evidence. 'I need to hold onto this. Vulpis wrote this for me.'

Theron turned on his heels before Martha could argue against it, and left for home. Theron leaned back against his car seat, head on the headrest, hands on the steering wheel. He sighed loudly.

'Damnit, Conor!'

When Theron arrived at his apartment, it was too early for the sun to rise but too late to call it night. Mrs Cassidy was already up. She was humming and sweeping the corridor.

'Morning, Mrs Cassidy.'

She inhaled loudly and put a hand to her heart. 'Oh, bless you, Theron. I know you've had a long night. I bet you, you were hunting that fox, Vulpis, again.'

'How did you guess?' Theron sarcasted.

Mrs Cassidy playfully slapped his arm. 'He's a wonderful man, and so dreamy. As are you. If I were thirty years younger . . .'

Theron was about to respond, genuinely flattered, and then stopped. He scowled. 'How do you know Vulpis is dreamy?' Theron agreed, but he wasn't going to tell *her* that.

'Because he came and brought me *this* just a little while ago.'

Theron's heart palpitated. Mrs Cassidy showed him a brooch that matched the description and images of the one that was stolen.

'That brooch is the one that was stolen from the jeweller's tonight.'

Mrs Cassidy gave Theron a pointed glare, chiding, 'It was stolen twenty years ago. It's a family heirloom, and Vulpis hunted it down for me. I gave him a picture of it years ago. He finally found it and returned it to me.'

Theron needed to process that.

'And before you go on about the legalities of it all, I have the paperwork to prove it – the receipt from when the brooch was first purchased sixty years ago when I was a child, and a police report that *I* filed when it was first stolen from me. That store was not in the know. Whoever stole it covered their tracks well.'

Theron blinked at her.

'What? You're not the only one who diligently follows the law.'

'Okay, then Vulpis and you should have come to me and reported it before he broke into that shop,' Theron pointed a thumb over his shoulder, 'and stole from that place, damaging the property. That's called vandalising.'

Mrs Cassidy put a hand on her hip, shifting her weight. 'You call him a lawbreaker. Tell me, does illegal always equate to immoral? Vulpis is a good man.'

He is! He was. I hope he still is. Theron shook himself from the thought.

'You're too hard on him. You need to soften up,' Mrs Cassidy went on.

Theron wanted the complete opposite for very different reasons. Again, Theron shook the thought away from his mind, banishing it completely.

He sighed. 'I'm glad you have your brooch back. Please come to the station tomorrow. We need to file that for our evidence.' Mrs Cassidy opened her mouth to protest. Theron added, 'Don't worry, we won't take it from you. We just need you to sign a few things.'

'Gladly.'

Mrs Cassidy returned to her sweeping and Theron walked to his apartment. Upon entering, he paused, sighing again. He passed a hand over his face.

'What am I going to do? I pined over you for so many years. I don't want to pine for you again now.'

As if answering his whispered plea, something knocked on his window. Scowling, Theron walked over, opening the drapes. There dangled a string with a rock tied to it – and a note.

Theron's heart leapt, thudded, and skipped several beats in syncopated rhythms.

'Fuck!' he breathed. Only Conor could ever have that effect on him.

Theron opened the window and grabbed the dangling rock that continued to clank against the glass. He nearly ripped the note in his hurry to free it. Theron realised he was smiling in anticipation. The note read, *Look up.*

Theron's heart pounded so hard. He stuck his head out and craned his neck up to see Conor flat on his stomach, dangling his arms over the edge of the roof. Conor waved at him, a wide grin on his face.

'Conor!'

'Hey, Theron. I missed you.'

'You! Fucking idiot!'

Conor's eyes widened at Theron's outburst.

'Do you realise that note could have gotten me into real trouble?'

'I thought you'd like it.'

'That's not the point!'

'So you like it?'

'You're so reckless!'

'You're such a stickler!'

Theron opened his mouth, working his jaw. 'I'm not having this argument here like this.'

He pulled inside and shut the window. He hurried out of his apartment and down the corridor to the stairs leading to the rooftop.

CHAPTER 3

Theron slammed the door open, marching onto the rooftop, where Conor waited for him, leaning against one of the large chimneys, arms and legs crossed, his hood down – grinning.

'What were you thinking?' demanded Theron, marching right up to him.

Conor pushed away from the chimney. 'I was thinking of *you*. I can't stop thinking about you.' Conor's face betrayed uncertainty.

'I have not once stopped thinking about you,' argued Theron.

'So what's the problem?'

'The problem! Is that you're Vulpis! A thief! A lawbreaker!'

'Or maybe! The problem! Is that you're a detective! A stickler! A pedant!'

The two men glared at each other, though there was no hatred behind the glower, only annoyance and incredulity. Conor was so much more handsome with his hood off, though Theron liked the Vulpis look too.

Theron shook his head, pointing behind him with his entire arm. 'Anyway, how did you find me? How did you know I lived here?'

'Mrs Cassidy told me. Kept going on about the handsome detective who's hunting me and how his heart is in the right place, but he just doesn't get it.' Conor placed a hand over his heart, chuckling. 'That and, if she were—'

'Thirty years younger,' Theron overlapped. Both of them chuckled.

Theron considered Mrs Cassidy's words about illegal not always being immoral.

'I guess you really did do her a solid tonight.'

Conor smiled fondly. 'She cried – when I gave her the brooch. She held it to her heart, clutching it. She kissed it. She kissed me.'

'She what?' Theron's response sounded like a threat.

'*On the cheek.*' Conor's open-mouth grin told Theron he enjoyed his jealousy.

Theron looked down. 'What *is* this, Conor? What are we?'

'I don't know. We're two men navigating meeting again after fifteen years and declaring the love we've always felt for each other. At least that's what it is to me.'

Theron met his gaze. 'That's what it is for me too.'

'So, where do we begin? How do we' – Conor gestured between them – 'figure this out?'

Theron shrugged, leaning his back against the large rectangular chimney. He folded his arms. 'I mean, it's not like I can't see past this, but we do have a major problem in that I am breaking all the rules right now just by talking to you and not reporting it in.'

Conor squinted in confusion. 'You didn't tell them you saw my face? That you know me?' Theron needn't answer, Conor knew. The thief grinned so widely, Theron had to avert his eyes. 'Theron! Are you breaking the law? I'm rubbing off on you.' Conor nudged Theron with his shoulder and the touch sent a tingle to his stomach.

Theron slid down to a crouch, sighing as his thoughts raced to wanting Conor to rub on him in very different ways. Conor joined him as the two sat on the gravel. They both placed their arms on their knees, sitting like they often did when they were teens.

'So what do you go by these days? Because I couldn't find you.'

Conor chuckled. 'You looked me up?' He laughed again. 'I switched around some of my names and changed my last name to my mother's maiden name.'

'Great.' Theron muttered in sarcasm, staring out towards the horizon. 'I was at it for hours, you know that?' He raised his voice in annoyance. 'Do you realise what you do to me, Conor? Coming back into my life after all these years, and then disappearing again? I have abandonment issues because of you.'

'I'm sorry.'

Theron hadn't expected Conor's tone to be so gentle, so sincere. He turned his head to stare at Conor.

'Let's start from the beginning. When did you realise you were in love with me?'

Conor's eyes twinkled. 'I think I knew when we were five. I was so drawn to you. Other friends were claiming who they'd marry, as far as a kid can tell these things. I wanted to be married to you. I never said it to you or to our other friends because I was scared to be an outcast.'

Conor stared out into the distance, across the roofs. 'When we were teens, I realised I had no attraction to girls whatsoever. I went to secret groups to become more assertive about being gay. I was scared to tell you because telling you I was gay also meant admitting to you you're the one who made me realise it.' He sighed, bowing his head. 'Now that I know . . . you know. I wish I had told you. I wanted to at that dance but I chickened out.' Theron realised they'd both nearly admitted their love on the same night and it clenched his heart. 'I wish I had told you you were breaking my heart with our friendship breakup because I loved you.'

'I wish you had too. Because I too chickened out at that dance.' Theron paused, pressing his lips together and feeling a mixed bag of emotions. 'I wish I had handled that differently – better. I just . . . couldn't face you leaving me. It was easier to hate you instead. But I regretted it. I pined over you for years.' Theron leaned his head back as he stared ahead. 'I knew I loved you since childhood too. It evolved and grew as we grew older and matured. I was attracted to girls too, they did things to me – to my heart, my body – but only you did the most.'

That got a grin from Conor.

'Are you seeing anyone?' Conor asked, turning to Theron.

Theron shook his head. 'You?'

'Neither. I . . . have commitment issues. I get scared that if I commit to someone, love them, they'll decide they hate me when something happens that is out of my control.'

It broke Theron's heart to hear that. 'I'm sorry.'

Conor shrugged. 'It's fine. I kept trying to make every guy like you, turn them into you, find you in them. But they could never be you. I thought for sure you would never feel the same way. It . . . it's amazing that you do.' The awe in Conor's voice moved Theron. 'You have no idea.'

'It's amazing that you feel that same way *I* do, and after all these years,' voiced Theron. A pang hit him. 'Do you forgive me? For that fight?'

'Yeah, I do.' Conor turned front again. 'There was this one guy, dark hair, bushy eyebrows like yours, blue eyes. He loved to talk dirty, like *raunchy* dirty.'

'Uh, okay?' The new pang that hit Theron was jealousy – again.

Conor chuckled. 'I told him to call me reckless while we were having sex.'

Theron stifled a laugh in his throat.

'I know. It was fun. It amused me. I enjoyed it, but it just wasn't the same as coming from you.'

Heart thudding, Theron turned his head to Conor. 'Are you telling me you want me to call you reckless when we have sex for the first time?'

'If you want.'

Theron's jaw dropped.

'I mean . . . I'm saying I like it when you call me reckless.' Conor blushed, turning his face away. 'And I wanna have sex with you.'

Heat rose to Theron's face. 'Same.' He paused before adding, 'Just not here on the roof. Seems a bit rough for my liking.'

Conor bit his lower lip, smiling, and looking up from under his eyelashes with bashful eyes.

'You know,' said Theron, 'I was always scared to be abandoned, so much that I could never fully commit much either. I . . . was engaged not too long ago, but it didn't work out.'

'What happened?'

'She cheated on me.'

'I'm sorry.'

'Nah, that was my fault – entirely. And you're the reason for it.'

'Me?' Conor got an amused glint in his eyes.

Theron shifted, sitting cross-legged and turning his body to face Conor. 'So here's the thing. Before hunting you down, hunting Vulpis, I was trying to move up in the firm. I think you leaving did that to me, wanting to hunt people down, search *mysteries*, not murderers but thieves and such. It reminded me of you somehow, without even knowing what you had become.' Theron chuckled.

It felt like they were 15 again, sharing everything that was on their hearts, except this time, they were being one hundred percent honest with each other about how they each felt for the other.

'I wished I could find you, but I couldn't.'

'You tried to find me again?' inquired Conor, brows creasing with chagrin.

'About a year after you moved, yeah.'

'I . . . had already changed my last name. I . . . it was weird, and still is a bit, with my family after coming out as gay. I tried different iterations before settling on one few would ever know once I became Vulpis.'

Theron nodded. 'My partner – detective partner – he was getting old when he had started hunting you. Took me on to help him and we thought we were making good headway, but you were always one step ahead of us. Sly fox as you are.'

Conor giggled, the side of his mouth curling up. 'Why do you think I chose Vulpis as my name?'

'When Barry retired, I continued, alone. I didn't want someone with me. We had been so inseparable, you and I, partners in everything, law and crime as teens, from shoplifting, to returning the goods to the police station.'

'I remember that,' laughed Conor, clapping his hands together in glee. 'You had me write a letter of apology to the shop owner and the police department.' Conor stuck out his tongue as he grinned widely, shimmying his shoulders. 'I guess being a stickler does have its merits, *they gave me a lollipop.*'

Theron rolled his eyes. 'Bet you wish *I'd* give you a lollipop.'

Conor leaned forward suddenly, and lingered, his lips so close, Theron could taste the smell of his breath. Theron's breath hitched.

'If only you knew how much.' Conor's voice was a purr that nearly made Theron melt.

'Conor,' breathed Theron, eyes darting between Conor's intense gaze and his lush lips.

Conor pulled away.

Theron blinked. 'You can't do that!' he protested, disappointment hitting him harder than he thought it would. 'Go in for a kiss and then pull away like that.'

'Sorry.' Conor hesitated. 'Now it's awkward.'

'Yeah, it is.'

The two of them shifted, quiet for a moment. Theron's racing heart calmed but slightly.

'So anyway,' Theron rubbed his forehead, trying to ignore the heat in his body. 'I got so enthralled by my work hunting Vulpis, I neglected my fiancée.'

'Who proposed?' asked Conor.

'She did. I accepted. My days weren't as lonely with her around, but I neglected her and she was lonely. One day, after coming so close to catching you I could smell you there . . .' Theron leaned in, breathing in through his nose. 'This smell, your leather outfit. I could smell it. I was so excited, had I known it was you then, might have explained why I was so bent on finding you, fixated on Vulpis, because I've been trying to find *you* this whole time.'

Conor nodded, sympathy on his features, which told Theron he understood what he meant.

Theron replayed the scene he was describing in his mind. He resumed. 'One morning after a long night hunting Vulpis, I found her and her other man in our bed.'

'Yikes.'

'I asked if he was treating her right. I asked if he made her happy and met her needs. And then . . . I invited them both to breakfast.'

'You what?' laughed Conor.

'I know, it's crazy, but I wanted them to know I bore no ill will towards them.' Theron shook his head, chuckling. 'I never looked back on that day ever again. I felt free. I felt like I could dedicate my life to . . . finding Vulpis.'

Conor's hand found Theron's in his lap and he interlaced their fingers. The tingles it generated were like sharing a first kiss with someone, but so much more.

They remained silent for a few minutes, relishing their touch as they enjoyed being in the present moment.

'How did it all start with Vulpis?' Theron asked, his voice gentle.

'Freshman year, college. A friend of mine got something very special to her stolen from one of the sorority girls. I volunteered myself to steel it back. We were a few to gather the evidence I needed. One of my friends was in the drama club. He got me a whole outfit, the first iteration of the Vulpis leathers – half medieval, half modern. I wanted a hood and he sewed it for me into the armour. I loved it.'

Conor's eyes grew distant. 'I admired myself in it, and it helped me assert my gayness even more. I snuck into that sorority house and took back the item. No one saw my face, but word spread. People started writing letters to the mystery thief through the college newsletter, describing items stolen and posting photos. Those items began popping back up – some I had to do more investigating for, some I sadly could not find. Few knew who I was, and I knew I wanted a good name. As I gained more skills, I came up with the name Vulpis.'

'Wish I'd been there. I almost feel jealous I didn't see your roots take shape.'

'See? You don't hate what I am.'

'I never said I did, I just said you were reckless and a lawbreaker,' insisted Theron.

Conor chuckled. 'After college, I just continued, I guess. Word kept spreading, and people never spoke of my identity to anyone, since what I stole now had more stakes and where I stole from too.'

'That sounds just like you, too,' Theron admitted.

He took Conor's other hand and interlaced their fingers too. Now, both hands thus locked, Theron bowed his head and Conor did the same. Sobering, they leaned their foreheads on each other.

'So what do we do about this? About us?' asked Theron.

'About me being Vulpis and you the detective hounding me?'

'Yeah.'

The answer was clear for both of them. *I don't know.*

Theron closed his eyes, relishing the moment. He breathed Conor in, the smell of his leathers, the smell of *him*. His heart leapt and his stomach tightened. They would have to go back to life – real life, not their past stories, not reminisces – and the reality was, Conor was a wanted thief and Theron was breaking rules by not bringing him in.

The sun rose on the horizon, a soft peach glow in the distance.

'I need to get home,' Conor said softly.

Theron's heart sank.

Conor stood, helping Theron up as well. The thief walked several paces ahead. He turned to face Theron, pointing a thumb behind him.

'I need to get home to Fidelis.'

Theron's heart sank further. He couldn't hide the roughness in his voice. 'I thought you said you weren't seeing anyone.'

Conor grinned, chuckling. 'Are you jealous?' He bit his lower lip. 'You're adorable when you get mad like that.'

Theron worked his jaw, unable to voice his protest.

'Fidelis is my *dog*.'

Theron felt like an idiot.

'She gets agitated when I come home too late, eager for a walk. We're in this lavish penthouse overlooking the lake of her favourite park. She's wonderful. When I found her, she was just a pup, abandoned, hungry.' His smile grew fond. 'I think she'd like you.'

'I'd like to meet her someday. Maybe soon.'

Conor marched to Theron, cupping his cheek with one hand, his gaze ablaze, the other hand on the small of Theron's back.

'I love you.'

Theron waited, heart pounding, hoping Conor would lean in for a kiss, but instead, he backed away, biting his lower lip, and winked, before he spun around, ran, and leapt over the edge of the roof to the next one.

Theron ran to the eave, watching Conor bound away, his heart leaping in just as many bounds, and his chest heaving.

CHAPTER 4

Conor was busy with several jobs. He wanted to go back to see Theron, but he knew it could prove dangerous – for both of them. He didn't want to put Theron into more trouble than he was probably already in.

Conor also enjoyed having the ball in his court and being chased by the man he loved. It thrilled him. Be that as it may, he longed for him.

Tucking the note he had for him in his pocket, hoping they'd come face to face on this job, Conor draped his hood over his head.

'It's been too long. A couple of weeks is too long.' Conor scratched Fidelis on the head before leaving the penthouse.

The job was simple, and he himself had tipped the detectives off. An anonymous caller, he had been. He chuckled with pride.

He waited on the rooftop for Theron to appear.

'Finally.'

Theron scowled. 'Were you waiting for me?'

'Who do you think tipped the station off?'

Theron gaped widely, pointing behind him. 'What would you do that for?! If you wanted to see me, why not just come see me?'

'I've been busy. I'm sorry.' As Conor continued, he took a few steps towards Theron. 'I didn't know how safe it was to return to your apartment, and I didn't want to put you into more trouble than was worth.'

'*You're* more trouble than is worth,' retorted Theron.

That hurt Conor. Theron must've noticed, for his expression softened. 'I'm sorry, I didn't mean it like that. I'm just tired of playing cat and mouse with you. Can we just *be* together already?'

Conor grinned, his heart leaping higher than it would when he jumped from roof to roof. He took a few more steps towards Theron.

'I'd like nothing more.' His voice was filled with yearning.

Theron perked up. 'So you're gonna let me take you in, then? We can try to figure things out from there.'

Conor's heart sank. He shook his head. Theron's face fell.

'Will you let me be who I am? Can we find a way to coexist with who we are?' Conor pointed to himself then at Theron, 'Thief and his hunter?'

Theron's brows furrowed as he closed the distance. 'Conor, I'm sorry. I'm taking you in, and we'll find a way from there. I need you to stop making me chase after you.' He spoke with earnestness. 'I need you.'

Conor cupped Theron's face. 'I need you too. I guess, maybe I like you chasing me. Because for so long, I thought you let me go. Because instead of hating me, I wished you'd tried to stop me from leaving.'

Both men sighed in sorrow. Conor's heart broke all over again at the memory. Then it leapt at the revelations they had revealed since.

He wanted to declare more, promise more, but a subtle click alerted him to Theron's next move. He quickly tugged his hand away, but the cuff wrapped around his wrist and closed.

Conor cursed, grabbing the other handcuff, and retaliated, wrapping it and his hands around Theron's wrist. The cuff closed as Conor backed Theron up and against the roof bulkhead, pinning him there.

Theron cursed, realising what Conor had done.

Heart thudding, Conor pressed himself against Theron, holding their cuffed wrists above the detective's head. Eyes darting to Theron's lips, Conor considered kissing him with abandon, and he bit his lower lip, wondering what Theron tasted like. By the look in Theron's vivid blue eyes, he craved the same.

Except there was that current small detail of being handcuffed together and police detectives below them who could walk in on them at any moment.

With his free hand, Conor reached into Theron's jacket to retrieve the key, stealthily slipping his note in at the same time. Then he lowered their cuffed hands and took a single step back.

'Conor,' Theron whispered.

Conor clicked his tongue, disappointed. He lifted the key.

'Shit, give that back.' Theron reached for it.

Conor pulled his hand out of reach. Acting on impulse, he lifted his arm back and tossed the key to the next roof over.

'Conor! What the hell?!'

Conor raised their cuffed wrists to eye level. 'You want it back? We gotta leap together.'

'I'm not a parkour expert like you, though!' Theron panicked.

'I taught you a trick that first night.'

'Yah, but . . . this is different. Plus, my team could come find us at any moment.'

'Then we better hurry.'

'Oh my . . . You're so reckless, Conor!' Theron seethed, though there was no hatred in his tone.

'You're the one who tried to cuff me, babe.'

Theron worked his jaw. Conor couldn't help but grin. He loved getting a rise out of Theron like that. Always had.

Conor bit his lower lip for a beat. 'For this to work, we need to take this leap together.'

'Are you referring to jumping to the next roof or are you referring to our relationship?'

'Both. But let's start by the roof.'

'Okay, that works.' Theron looked relieved and disappointed at once. It was a look he'd often have when they were younger. And now Conor knew why.

Conor led Theron to the eave. 'This roof is flat, no gravel, it'll be easier to jump. Legs extended like a ballerina, okay? We run together and jump together. When we land, we roll forward to cushion our fall.'

Theron's earnest eyes met Conor's. 'I'm scared.'

'About the jump or about us?'

'Both.'

That made Conor's heart thud. 'I need you to trust me.'

Theron nodded.

Conor backed up, Theron followed. Conor took a deep breath. 'Lean forward to give your body momentum.' Theron merely nodded, swallowing. Conor wanted his lips on Theron's mouth so badly, but right now, they had a jump to succeed together before someone caught them on the roof like this. For Theron, he was doing this.

'You're so impulsive,' Theron whispered.

Conor laughed. 'So are you.'

Theron scowled as though pondering. Then muttered half-committedly, 'True.'

Conor was glad Theron recognised at least that. 'In some ways, we're the same.'

'You must be rubbing off on me.'

'And yet, my last jobs, I left receipts that prove what I was stealing was going to the rightful owners. You must be rubbing off on *me*.'

'Or did Mrs Cassidy inspire you?'

'Oh, she had receipts?' Conor honestly had no idea that she had. He had just seen the images and hunted down her brooch. For two years he'd been searching for it for her.

'Let's get this over with.' Theron sighed, 'You really test me, Conor.'

Conor remembered something from their childhood. 'You're not a heights guy, are you? I remember you getting nervous when we climbed trees.'

'*Now* you remember that detail.'

'You still come onto roofs for me, climb up here to find me?' Conor turned to Theron, wanting to kiss him right then. And ready to do it. 'You're afraid of heights,' he stepped closer to Theron, his voice turning husky, 'and yet you've been following me up on roofs and even jumped the gap for me.'

'There is a lot I've been doing for you for a lot longer than I consciously realised, Conor.' The tone in Theron's voice matched Conor's.

'There is a lot I've been doing for you too, Theron, longer than I consciously realised.'

Conor took a quick moment to allow himself to admire Theron's features, his eyes, his lips, and to feel all that he felt for him. He decided they'd do this jump first before they did anything else.

As though linked telepathically, they both turned back to face the adjacent roof. 'Okay, ready?'

'As I'll ever be.'

'One, two, three! Run!'

They bounded towards the edge of the roof and leapt over to the next one, wind on their faces, time stopping, and rolled forward as they landed, almost in tandem, getting a bit tangled in each other's limbs as they stopped.

Theron laughed. 'We did it!'

'I'm so proud of you.' Detangling themselves, Conor rose, as did Theron. Their cuffed hands instinctively interlaced.

Theron beamed at Conor, his other hand on Conor's arm. 'Conor, darling, we did it, we jumped!'

'How do you feel?'

'That was . . .' Theron was out of breath. His next word came out husky. 'Exhilarating.'

Conor's knees nearly buckled at Theron's tone. He knew he would melt in his arms when they did get their chance to be intimate together.

Conor motioned with his head. 'And there is our key.' He started for it and paused. He grinned at Theron. 'Darling?'

Theron shrugged, smiling fondly. 'It just came out.'

Conor bit his lip before answering with tenderness. 'I like it.' Conor bent, lifting one leg behind him as he picked up the small key. He handed it to Theron. 'Want to do the honours?'

Theron took the key and unlocked the handcuffs. A small tinge of disappointment hit Conor as they pulled their hands away from each other.

Voices alerted Conor to Theron's colleagues approaching and their time being cut short. He backed away.

'I'll see you in a few, babe.'

Conor leapt down to a balcony and swung himself over to the lower roof. He looked back up to see Theron's face light up as he read the note Conor had left him. He bit his lower lip, excited and giddy.

* * *

Feeling like they had just shared an intimate moment, Theron watched Conor bound down, putting his hands in his pockets. That's when he felt it. Theron pulled out the note. It was written in that same delicate handwriting on a piece of that same kind of lovely stationery.

Theron's heart did something. Moments ago he felt a tinge of disappointment but now . . . *Meet me on the roof of the Lakeshore Hotel at 8 p.m. in three days' time.*

Theron brought the note to his heart as he looked afar, watching Conor's form become smaller as he disappeared on the horizon of rooftops.

Chapter 5

Conor fixed his collar as he sat waiting. He was so nervous. He hoped Theron understood to dress up – this was a date, a real first date. Conor wanted it to be perfect. They had yet to figure things out, but Conor wanted this so badly.

He had reserved the entire rooftop. His line of work allowed him that much luxury to splurge from time to time.

The mood was set to gentle lights, a fountain sparkled nearby, and the effervescence of changing colours added to the setting. Conor had picked gentle music from a lounge band both he and Theron had enjoyed when they were teens.

As for himself, he was clean-shaven and dressed in a lavish pale beige suit, with a cufflink flower in his suit's jacket pocket. The suit was warm enough for the cool night but cool enough to wear during warmer seasons too.

Conor's palms grew clammy. He never got nervous like this for a job. It was the first time he was this scared. He was scared Theron wouldn't show up.

Footsteps alerted him to someone approaching. Conor's heart skipped a beat. There walked Theron. His thin and subtle goatee was even better kept than usual, and he was dressed in a simple yet elegant charcoal suit, the top two buttons of his shirt unbuttoned.

'Theron, you came.' Conor stood to meet him.

'Yeah.' Theron stopped in front of Conor.

'You look hot.' They both said. Conor laughed.

Theron hesitated, looking just as nervous as Conor felt. 'You chose that band we liked to relax to.'

Conor nodded. 'I'm relieved you recognise them.'

'Conor, I couldn't stop listening to them because I'd listen to them with you. I was obsessed. And then, after you left, if I listened to them, I bawled my eyes out, so I stopped.'

Conor let out a shaking breath – that hit him with a pang. He offered his hand to Theron, who took it. Conor led him to their table.

Theron looked around. 'Are we the only patrons?'

Conor felt bashful about all he'd done for this date. 'I reserved the place. Someone owed me a favour.' It was partially true, though he had splurged for it too.

Theron smiled tenderly. 'Darling, it's lovely. Thank you for arranging this for us. For . . . our first official date.'

Conor smiled, beginning to feel more relaxed.

The waiter brought them some champagne and poured it for them.

'This is fancy.' Theron took his glass and held it up.

Conor tilted his glass forward, inviting Theron to a toast.

'What are we toasting to?' inquired Theron.

'To us, I guess. Finding each other. Admitting our feelings. Everything.'

Theron's smile sent warmth to Conor's stomach. As Conor sipped, he glanced at Theron, the knots loosening.

They chatted for a while, both nervous, until the main course arrived. Then they were busy devouring the food.

'This is so good,' said Theron. 'You remember that time your mom tried to make Filet Mignon but it burnt?'

Conor laughed. 'And it looked like rocks of carbon.' He clapped his hands. 'And we still ate it.'

'Hey, the inside was fine. I liked it.' Theron grinned, then covered his mouth to hide the food he was chewing.

Conor suppressed a laugh, feeling giddy.

After the meal, Conor stood, wiping his mouth with his cloth napkin. He offered his hand to Theron.

'Oh, got somewhere you want to take me?' Theron took Conor's hand and stood.

Conor led Theron a little ways away. Their song began to play as Conor held Theron's hand in his, placing his other hand on the small of his back.

Theron's eyes lit up. 'You remembered our song?'

'Of course, babe.' Conor bit his lower lip. 'That dance where we both chickened out declaring our love, the first school dance we dared to go to, we tried to get dates but that was a no-go.'

'Every guy was paired up with a girl, dancing,' said Theron. 'And the girl I had asked turned me down to dance with that hotshot.'

'Yeah, and to comfort you, I offered to dance with you.' Conor brought their clasped hands to his heart.

Theron's cheeks flushed. 'No one ever said anything to us about that.'

'No, eh,' Conor realised. 'It was the most free I had felt in a long time.' He lifted Theron's hand to his lips and brushed a tender kiss to his knuckles.

'And there I thought you were dancing with me just to make me laugh.'

Conor and Theron moved in tandem, slowly shuffling in circles to the gentle music.

'That dance meant everything to me,' Conor said softly.

Conor leaned the side of his forehead on Theron's, their cheeks touching. He closed his eyes.

'I never wanted it to end,' whispered Theron.

Conor let out an airy groan, tightening his hold. Theron's lips found Conor's neck. Conor's breath hitched. He pressed his cheek more on Theron's and kissed him just below the ear.

'Conor,' Theron whispered.

'Theron.'

Their hands travelled the lengths of their bodies as their dance turned into an exploration of each other.

Exhaling a euphoric sigh, Conor slipped his hand under Theron's shirt, relishing touching him. Their mouths angled closer, lips nearly touching. It was so elating. Conor gasped, as did Theron, and they tightened their grips on each other, their lips still too far apart. They pressed themselves closer, their embrace turning even more intimate.

Conor leaned in, lips parting, ready to share his first kiss with Theron.

Theron stepped away quickly, just before their lips could touch. 'I can't.'

Conor's breath caught in his throat.

'I'm sorry.'

'Too fast? Too public?'

Theron shook his head. 'Too perfect.' Theron looked so sad, so apologetic. 'You did this all for me, but I just . . . not until we've figured this out, figured *us* out, because at the end of the day, we're still hunter and thief.'

A wave of emotions threatened to overwhelm Conor. He had to turn his face away as his eyes blurred with tears.

'This doesn't change how I feel about you. I still want us to be together. I still want us to make this work. I just need to figure some things out, so that we *can* make it work.'

Conor shut his eyes tightly. 'I am trying to meet you halfway, just so you know.'

'I'm trying too. But right now, I don't see a way past this.'

Conor pressed his eyes more tightly as tears ran from them, his jaw clenching in a silent sob.

'I need to figure out how and what, so that we can get past this hurdle that is who and what we are.'

Conor nodded, eyes still shut, unable to do anything else.

It was Theron's turn to cup Conor's cheek. Conor breathed in sharply, eyes flying open. Theron gently turned Conor's face towards him and wiped a tear with his thumb.

'Darling,' Theron whispered. 'I love you.'

Conor let out a shaking breath, a weep for the man he loved.

They stayed like that for a minute before Theron pulled his hand away; Conor's cheek felt cold in its absence. Theron leaned in and gently pecked a kiss on Conor's cheek before backing away.

Conor watched Theron leave, his heart aching. He brought a fist to his mouth to clamp down the sob that might have been too loud.

He realised something was sticking out of his chest pocket. Conor pulled out a note. It was written in Theron's handwriting.

Conor wiped his eyes to clear the blur of tears away. *I'm serious about wanting us to make this work.* And he had left his phone number.

'Babe,' whispered Conor, bringing the note to his mouth and kissing it. He closed his eyes, smelling Theron on the piece of paper.

<u>CHAPTER 6</u>

Theron marched into Martha's office and shut the door behind him. The middle-aged woman looked up from her computer screen with a puzzled expression as Theron began to pace.

'I need to tell you something off the record,' he began.

Martha clasped her hands together, leaning against the back of her chair. 'I'm listening.'

Theron stopped and faced his boss. 'I know his identity – Vulpis.' Martha waited, obviously deducing there was more. 'You know that friend who got away? The one I always wished . . .' Theron steeled himself for her reaction. 'It's him.'

Martha nodded slowly. 'I take it your relationship with him since finding this out has been . . . complicated at best.'

Theron sighed, 'You don't know the half of it, Martha.' Theron brought his hands to his head. 'He told me he's in love with me.'

'And you feel the same way?'

Theron brought his hands down. 'If I don't, it's only because what I feel is so much more intense.' He lifted his arms in frustration. 'We haven't even kissed and we're making love declarations.' He pulled the chair out and sat down, leaning forward, arms on his knees. 'It's such a mess, Martha. If I knew half the things I know now back then . . .'

Martha was quiet for a few beats.

'I know he meant a lot to you. I hadn't realised you felt so strongly for each other.'

'Neither did I. Neither did *we*.' Theron bowed his head. 'I love him, Martha. Always have.'

'I suppose it was always evident in a way. You might have denied it to yourself, and I might not have caught on to the full intensity of what you felt, but it was obvious this friend of yours had either been a love interest or like family.'

'And now he's the thief I've been after all these years, the thorn in my side.' Theron looked at Martha, pleading. 'Why does he have to be so reckless? Why does he have to be Vulpis? I want to be with him, but I don't know how.' Theron deflated even more. 'I hope you're not pissed that I didn't come to you sooner. I'm still . . . processing it all.'

Martha, to Theron's surprise, offered him a sympathetic smile. 'I get it. And it's not like he's a bad person. He's a lawbreaker, and we've been after him, trying to catch him, but he's never killed anyone, he's never done anything cruel. All he's ever done is thieving and breaking into places.'

'If it weren't for that, he'd be perfect.'

Martha let out a laugh. 'Love isn't perfect, Theron, I can tell you that. You think my husband and I are in constant bliss? He drives me insane sometimes.' She folded her arms. 'But I'd be lost without him. And you look like you've just been found while trying to navigate the complications of all that it implies.'

Martha had not once reprimanded Theron. For his part, the detective *had* talked Martha's ear off about Conor throughout the years. It was no wonder she wasn't faulting him for not having been honest with her about it sooner. And *it* – as Martha said it, with her tone – implied the situation, Theron and Conor's love, Vulpis, everything.

Martha leaned forward. 'I've been reading the tabloids. People are in love with Vulpis. There's gotta be a way we can meet halfway, him and us.'

That meant more to Theron than he could ever express to Martha. Theron was coming to her because he trusted her and needed help figuring this out, and she was willing to offer that for him.

'I tried. I don't know.' Theron shook his head. 'I also – before you ask – looked him up. No go. He had, like, three middle names, both his parents had two sur-names. I tried every combination I could think of. He changed his name – it was legal, as far as he claims. And I believe him. I doubt he'd go out of his way to create a new identity. Else he wouldn't have this Latin nickname. From what I know of him then and now, he found a loophole somewhere.'

'Then let's start with that to track him down. The loopholes.' She paused but a beat. 'We need to catch him, something's gotta give. But if he's willing to talk, then so am I.'

Theron nodded. He waited a bit but Martha said nothing more and turned back to her computer. Theron internally was grateful that she didn't inquire anything more about how many times he and Conor had seen each other or how long Theron had known who Vulpis was.

Theron stood and walked to the office door.

'Theron?'

Theron looked over his shoulder.

'We'll find your solution. So we can stop him *and* so that you can be with him.'

Theron frowned. 'Won't that land him in jail?'

'Not if we find something in the law. He'll have to meet us partway. But I know there's something in there.'

'Thank you.' Theron was overcome with emotion, he had to blink back his tears. 'Thanks for being understanding.'

'Only if it'll shut you up about him and put a permanent smile on your face,' Martha teased, a smirk on the corner of her mouth. 'Ever since you've been part of this firm you haven't stopped going on about this guy. I have the whole backstory. And I've got your back.'

'You're the best boss I could have asked for.'

'Yeah, yeah, remember that the next time you decide to keep information from me for who knows how many weeks or months.'

Theron suppressed a smile. 'Yes, ma'am.'

Theron exited, shutting the office door behind him. His heart was doing somersaults in his chest. Theron hadn't looked over any legal documents or read through laws in ages, but he would do it. He chuckled to himself as he returned to his desk. Only for Conor.

* * *

'He drives me insane!' Conor shouted, practically pulling his hair out. He paced quickly, looking up at the ceiling. 'He just . . .' He stopped. 'He's so stuck up. He's such a stickler. You don't get more law-abiding than him! He can't see past the stupid laws!'

On the floor, Fidelis tilted her head to the side. Conor sighed and plopped onto the sofa. 'I don't know what to do, Fidelis. I'm so in love with him. How are we going to get past this? What solution are we going to find?'

The dog jumped onto the sofa and sat down beside Conor, placing her head on his lap, offering him a short whimper of sympathy. Conor instinctively began stroking her mane.

'I just wish he'd look beyond the law and see me for what I do and the *good* I do.' Conor closed his eyes. 'I think he does, but he's so set in his ways. Law this, law that. Urrrrgh!' Conor leaned forward, bowing his head. 'I just want to *be* with him. But I don't want to change who I am. I *can't* change who I am, Fidelis. This is me. I want him to accept that.'

The dog made a throat sound.

'Yeah, maybe I *am* overthinking things. Maybe he does accept me, but his stupid laws are preventing him from moving forward.' Conor leaned back. 'Reckless. Reckless! he calls me.'

Conor sighed, thinking hard. Theron had always followed all the rules, every single law, ever since they had known each other as kids.

'That's it!'

Conor grabbed his laptop. Fidelis tilted her head with a question in her soft sound.

'I just need to find a loophole in the law. Something that can allow us to be together, despite everything. Theron wants to follow the law, so I'm going to find the law that allows us to be together, that will let me continue to help people the way I do best, and will respect his need for rules to be obeyed.'

Conor realised that while he felt Theron might want him to change, *he* was hoping *Theron* would change. That was going to get them nowhere. They had to meet part way. They were both trying, Conor knew, but maybe they weren't looking in the right places.

Conor began typing and stopped short. 'I don't even know what I'm supposed to be searching!'

Conor had not read any legal documents in so long, and the last time he did, all the legalese had him using a dictionary for more than half the words he read. He chuckled, murmuring to himself.

'Only for you, Theron.'

* * *

Conor needed a break. He dialled and hung up five times before he let it ring. He almost chickened out and hung up again, but then Theron answered.

'Theron Morin.'

Conor suppressed a laugh. He'd never heard Theron so terse and all-business. He bit his lower lip.

'Hello?'

'Hey,' Conor said gently.

'Conor!'

The two fell silent.

'I've been thinking . . .' They both stopped.

'About you,' Theron completed, his tone tender. 'I was hoping you'd call.'

'Now that I've called, you know my number so you can call me anytime too.' Conor hesitated, wondering if he should tell Theron what he'd been searching for, even if he'd found nothing yet. He glanced at the dictionary that lay open near his laptop on the coffee table. 'Someone wants to say hi.'

Conor called Fidelis to him. 'Come here, girl.' The dog happily barked.

'Hi, Fidelis,' Theron said through the phone.

'Say, you wanna video call?' Conor asked tentatively.

In response, Theron's video popped up on Conor's screen. Theron was standing, leaning against the wall. He was so handsome, Conor was beginning to regret asking, for it made the longing so much more intense.

Conor activated his camera. Theron's eyes grew earnest.

'It's good to see you.' Theron scratched his forehead. 'Look, I'm sorry about how I left things the other night. The date was perfect. I just . . . I want this to work – us. I want to find what I can to make it work. I'm not losing you again, Conor. I'm not gonna risk sneaking around with you, afraid of you getting arrested and taken from me all over again. I can't bear it. I'm going to find how we can be together, safely, and . . . permanently.'

Conor was so moved. 'Theron, that just reassured so many fears and answered so many questions.'

Theron smiled. He sat down. On his desk sat a strange orb.

Conor smirked. 'Is that the crystal ball I gave you as a joke the year before I moved away?'

Theron opened his mouth, glancing at the thing, and blushed.

'Oh, my god, I can't believe you kept that thing.'

'I . . . it was all I had left of you.' Theron took the orb and brought it to his bosom, stroking it as though it were a cat. 'Will Conor let me see his pet?' Theron looked down. 'It tells me yes.'

'You know that can be interpreted in a very different way.'

Theron snorted his laugh.

'Had I known, I would have slipped into your office when I broke into the place,' teased Conor.

'That would've been one way for you to learn I was hunting you.'

'Or just worked with my hunter.' Conor tapped his thigh. 'Hey, Fidelis, come here, girl. Come say hi to Theron.' Fidelis jumped onto Conor hard, pressing on his stomach. 'Oof.' She yapped happily, wagging her tail.

'Aw, she's adorable.'

Conor leaned back, lying down on his couch and crossed his legs. He and Theron continued to chat – it almost felt like they were a normal couple. Every time Conor thought that during the conversation, he bit his lower lip. When he did, something in Theron's eyes made him seem so much more enticing. Conor realised they were reacting to each other.

After a time, not long enough of chatting, Theron said, 'Gotta go. Boss is calling a meeting.' He hesitated. 'Conor. I love you.'

Conor smiled. 'I love you too, Theron.'

Theron hung up.

Grinning as he bit his lip, Conor brought his phone to his chin, feeling wistful.

* * *

Theron brought his phone to his heart, smiling and yearning. 'I should have let him kiss me,' he whispered to himself. He kicked himself internally for pulling away so soon. Their date was so perfect. He was so awed Conor had done all that for him.

Theron sighed.

When he reached Martha's office, he noted everyone else who was present.

'We've got a hit on Vulpis's next location and target.' That had Theron's heart drumming faster. Martha gave Theron a pointed look. 'Are you good to lead the team in?'

'Yes.'

'I assume Vulpis will not be willing to come in to speak with us if we asked politely.' Again Martha gave Theron those wide eyes that told him this was her coded way of telling him she understood his situation and position. And was verifying with him.

Theron turned to the group. 'When we go in, we don't shoot. We try to corner him, capture him, stun him at worst. *No one* shoots unless I give the command. Understood?'

CHAPTER 7

The night had come to move in on the location where Vulpis would strike – a museum on the city outskirts. Theron tried calling Conor on the way over but it went straight to voicemail. He had already left *several* messages. They had spoken once since the other day and Conor had assured Theron he would be gone by the time they moved in.

But something wasn't right, Theron just felt it.

Usually, when someone tipped them off, they gave the time they estimated Vulpis would be there. Conor always managed to get away quickly, but if someone gave an earlier time to trap Vulpis . . . By now Theron knew Conor worked within the hour and usually would go in sometime between one and three in the morning.

The tipper told them to be there at midnight. It just didn't feel right to Theron. Everyone was fidgety and there was no sign of Conor when they arrived.

Theron knew Martha wasn't testing him because she voiced her concerns to him in private and worried someone in the team had it out for Vulpis. They shared the same concern. Besides, Martha cared about her detectives and agents, and she cared about Theron enough to want to help him find a solution. She too had been looking into legalities.

Theron stepped aside and tried Conor again. He fell on his voicemail again. *You know who you've reached. You know what to do.*

Theron spoke in a frantic whisper. 'Darling, it's me. Something's not right. Don't come tonight. I know you've got a job, but don't do it. Forget it and come another night.'

Theron hung up. He just couldn't shake that feeling. A rock formed in the pit of his stomach.

The agents positioned themselves and they entered the building. Theron took the lead, gun held up in case someone else was there to surprise attack them. The place was dark, aside from some amber security lights here and there.

Theron walked up the stairs to the second floor. He wondered if he should go to the roof and stop Conor from entering the building.

He was the first one on the scene, as the others were still on the first floor.

Something screeched, like nails on a chalkboard, and then the glass of a window broke off clean.

So that's how he does it, Theron realised.

Conor held a card of sorts, but Theron could see the gleam that marked it as a knife disguised as a credit card. And then Conor placed a protector over it – which Theron approved of, relieved Conor wasn't reckless enough to carry such a sharp weapon without ensuring he didn't hurt himself with it.

Conor leapt into the building through the window, landing softly on both feet. Theron drew in a breath to shout his warning when someone behind him shouted. 'It's Vulpis!'

'Shit!'

Conor's eyes widened when he saw Theron. Theron shook his head. Conor turned heel and ran the way he'd come, ready to leap back out of the window.

A gunshot thundered in the quiet space and Theron's heart sank.

Conor cried out just as he leapt out of the museum, droplets of blood staining the floor.

'No!' cried Theron. He spun on his team. 'What part of "you don't shoot unless I give the command" did you not understand!?' His eyes narrowed on Lorenzo, whose gun was still smoking. Theron turned to the rest of the team. 'I want a perimeter sweep. Call every hospital and ask for a man dressed in black leathers injured on his left side, anywhere on the left side, gunshot wound.'

Theron didn't wait for acknowledgement. He turned and began to run. He found the security stairs and sprinted up to the highest floor. He searched for the emergency roof exit and ran outside. The wind whipped past his face, it was blowing hard.

'Vulpis! *Vulpis!*' he cried.

Theron dashed to the edge of the roof. Another droplet of blood stretched by the wind lay on the ground.

'Oh god,' he breathed, a hand on his mouth. His eyes blurred with tears. He was so scared for Conor's life right now.

Theron holstered his gun and took several steps back. He gave himself the momentum he needed and ran, leaping to the next rooftop. His fear for Conor made him forget his fear of heights.

He looked around for Conor, shouting out his coded name.

'VULPIS!'

Panicked, Theron brought his hands to his hair. 'Think, think, where would Conor go? He'd stick to the rooftops as much as possible. Where would he go? Would he go home?'

Theron had to try. He didn't know where Conor lived and that cold sensation hit his stomach even harder.

Then he remembered.

'Penthouse overlooking a lake and a park.'

Theron ran from roof to roof, a little slower than he knew Conor to be, but Conor was slowed down by an injury. Theron followed the trail he thought Conor would have taken, the logical route, confirmed every time he found a drop of blood, until he reached some tall complexes overlooking a park. He found the one overlooking the lake, and knew he could search those apartments on that side of the building.

His chest felt tight as fear kept gripping him, he was out of breath from running, scaling, parkouring, and he kept feeling on the verge of a full blown panic attack – because of his fear for Conor *and* his fear of heights.

Luckily for him, despite being far lower than any penthouse, there were emergency stairs and ladders at the back of each of the buildings.

Theron managed to scale his way to the roof. He found more droplets of blood – they were scarce. This meant Conor wasn't bleeding too much, or he was just that fast. But the few drops he'd seen along the way told Theron Conor had gone straight home.

Theron saw a larger pool of blood near one edge and figured Conor had come down from there.

Fearfully, tentatively, Theron peered over the eave of the roof and was relieved to find a balcony with light coming from inside. He jumped down.

Conor looked up, startled, a bandage on his arm, blood staining it but not too much. He had removed his top leathers and wore a simple black T-shirt. Conor gaped at Theron whose chest heaved, he was breathing so heavily.

Theron swung the patio door open – thankful it was unlocked – and entered Conor's apartment.

'How did you . . . ?'

'I followed the trail of blood.' Theron panted. 'I remembered . . . penthouse . . . overlooking a lake and park . . .'

'Did you parkour your way here?' Conor seemed more concerned about Theron than he did about his arm.

Theron nodded. He bent, a dizzy spell hitting him hard as black dots danced in his vision. He took in a large lungful of air.

'Babe!'

Theron pointed at Conor from this position. 'Only for you.' He breathed heavily. 'You reckless idiot! The things I do for you.' Theron rose. 'You should get that checked.'

'I'm fine. I put adhesive sutures. This isn't the first time I injure myself.'

'You didn't *injure* yourself,' cried Theron, exasperated at Conor. 'Don't be reckless, Conor. You were shot at!'

'By your team!' Conor shouted back.

'I never gave the order to. I knew something was off. Did you not get my messages?'

'I never bring my phone with me on a job.'

Theron felt like his lungs were squeezing and he couldn't bring air in them. 'Conor, I'm so scared for you right now. You need to get that looked at.'

'The bullet only grazed me. I'm okay. I bled as I ran because my heart was pumping. I placed those sutures. I'm okay, for real. I've had worse.'

Theron merely gaped at Conor.

'You swear you didn't—?'

'No! I wanted to warn you. Something felt off. I don't know what. I promise you.' Theron put his hands to his hair as tears stung his eyes.

'Why did you run along the roofs? You hate heights. You could have taken your car.'

'I needed to follow your trail. I needed to find you.' Theron felt desperate. He shouted his emotions. 'Conor. I worry about you, I need you safe. I can't do this anymore! I can't take this distance. I came to find you because I can't – do – this!'

'Can't do us?' Conor asked, his voice cracking.

'NO! I can't do the *not us* or is-it-us thing.' Theron shouted even louder. 'I need us to find a way for this to work and just *be* together because it's – you're – driving me mad, because you're so fucking reckless and right now I don't care! I want to be reckless too because you're the love of my life!'

A beat passed as they heaved before they both lunged forward, lips locking in a fiery kiss that had been far too long coming. Theron sob-moaned into Conor's mouth just as Conor did into Theron's. Their hands wrapped around each other as their tongues twined.

It felt like such a relief, like Theron could breathe again. Theron gripped the back of Conor's neck as Conor squeezed Theron closer to him, pressing them together.

Raking his hand through Conor's hair, Theron felt the same burning passion and desire he felt every time the two of them had come close to kissing, but so much more intense, and he moaned, expressing his need. Conor responded in kind, taking a few steps forward, cupping Theron's face and leading him towards the bedroom.

Locked in their passionate embrace, they tore each other's clothes off.

'I love you, Conor.'

'I love you, Theron.'

And their lips were back on each other's, devouring. Theron fell back onto the bed, Conor on top of him, both of them ready to experience their love physically and intimately. And their declarations culminated as the two made love for the first time.

* * *

Theron pressed his lips hard on Conor's, trying and failing to suppress a sob. Conor wept too. Now as the heat came down, they held each other tightly.

'I want to forget everything and just be with you tonight.'

'You're with me, babe. You're with me.'

Theron propped himself up on his elbow, wiping his eyes. 'And you're certain that doesn't need professional dressing?'

'Theron, my arm is fine. I promise. We just had the most amazing sex of my life and it didn't bleed.'

'Right.' Theron felt silly. 'I just worry – because you're so reckless.'

Conor bit his lower lip, the sorrow on his face being replaced by tenderness. 'I love it when you tell me that.'

So Theron repeated, leaning in towards Conor more each time. 'You're reckless, darling. My darling, Conor. My darling, Vulpis. You're so reck-less.' He completed with a quick but tender kiss.

They both chuckled. Theron lay back down and took a deep breath in, relishing the smell of his lover.

'So we're official?' Conor asked gently.

'I'd like us to be.'

'Same.'

'Then, we're official.'

* * *

Conor awoke not in Theron's arms like they had fallen asleep. He moved to find that his hand was handcuffed to the bed.

Theron was dressed and sitting on the chair in front of the bed, scrolling through his phone.

Conor propped himself up. 'What's the meaning of this?' Theron looked up from his phone. Conor moved his cuffed hand, causing a clink. 'Judging by your dressed self, this isn't a kink thing.'

Conor was still naked and felt trapped and exposed in ways that had nothing to do with his state of undress.

Theron stood and took a step forward. 'Darling,' his voice was a warning and Conor didn't like that. 'I think I found our solution, but it requires you to come to the station with me and—'

'You're apprehending me?' Conor cried in disbelief, his heart sinking.

'Well, I was worried you'd try to run away before hearing me out, so—'

'So what, you just wanted to *use* me and—'

'No, I promise, I just . . .'

Tears stung Conor's eyes.

Theron continued at a rapid pace. 'I think I found a solution, but I was scared you might not want to hear it. I was scared you'd be reckless again and leave. I . . . was scared you were going to leave me.' Theron suddenly blinked back tears to no avail and Conor understood. Theron bowed his head. 'As I've said, I . . . have abandonment issues.'

Conor's heart clenched as anger rose inside him for having followed his parents, feeling powerless as he had been to protest against it.

'I wish I would have told them no, refused to move. And *stayed*. It hurt me, it hurt you.' Conor's breath shook at the sheer emotions both he and Theron felt, realising how much he loved Theron, how his love was so much more intense than he initially thought, especially now, after having made love to each other. 'You're going to have to trust me.'

'You're right. I'm sorry.' Theron stepped forward and uncuffed Conor. Tossing the handcuffs aside, he took a step back, his arms fidgeting at his sides. He met Conor's gaze, eyes glistening, and whispered, 'Please don't leave me. I can't bear to lose you again.'

Conor pulled Theron to him, a hand on his back, the other cupping his cheek, and kissed him with such heat, it took his own breath away. His hand glided up Theron's side and came to rest on his other cheek. Theron gasped through the kiss, and moaned before sobbing.

Conor's lips parted from Theron's slowly. He leaned his forehead on his hunter's. 'Theron, I have no intention of ever leaving your side again.'

Theron exhaled a tearful whimper.

'I love you.' Conor held Theron's face firmly in both hands. 'I want to commit to you. I *am* committed to you.' He let out a one-breathed laugh. 'I'm the reckless one? And here you go cuffing me as though to cause another fight. Please don't do that, cause us to fight. Just be honest with me . . . and trust me.'

'Then I ask the same of you,' Theron replied gently. 'I . . . we need to go speak with Martha. I think I found a loophole in the law that will allow us both to continue what we do best, without you going to jail, but we need Martha's stamp of approval.'

Conor studied Theron's face, worried this might be a trap, but he recognised the longing in both Theron's eyes and in his own heart, and knew. 'Okay.'

CHAPTER 8

'Thank you for trusting me.' Theron said as the two got into his car.

Conor had dressed formally for the occasion, as had Theron in his usual detective suit. As a safety measure, under the snug-fitting black suit, Conor wore his Vulpis leathers.

Conor reached towards him and squeezed his hand. 'I'm willing to do this compromise for you.'

That meant the world to Theron. His face became hot and his vision blurred.

'Babe,' whispered Conor.

Theron couldn't stop his tears from spilling out, as though a dam had broken. And as he let it all out, Conor's eyes reflected his understanding and mirrored emotions, sparkling with tears.

'I just, every time . . . It hurt so much when you left fifteen years ago and I was so scared and lonely. I can't lose you again. You're the love of my life, I've always loved you. I don't care anymore that you're Vulpis, I just want us to be together. I don't want anyone taking you away from me. I need you so much.'

Conor wrapped his arms around Theron, and the two of them held each other, weeping in silence for a moment.

'I was so heartbroken,' whispered Conor. 'I've always loved you too. You're the love of my life too.' He held Theron more tightly. 'I need us to be together, always. I hurt when I'm not with you. I ache for you every day. I have ached for you for years, even when we were best friends, because I loved you and didn't know that you loved me too.'

They both heaved, their mouths drawing close and they shared a series of fiery kisses before pulling away from each other.

Theron wiped Conor's cheek with his thumb as Conor cupped Theron's face.

Theron needed to be certain. 'And you're serious about this?'

'I'm serious about *us*.' Conor's gentle reply fluttered Theron's heart.

'Darling, my promise to you is to trust you and be with you, and not let anything get in the way of that ever again. For as long as I live.'

'My promise to you is to trust you and be honest and never leave your side, for as long as I live.'

They kissed again, the comfort of Conor's soft lips filling Theron with elation. He breathed out a small spasm, blushing as he realised he'd totally make love again now if they could.

'Just know that,' Conor added, peering into Theron's eyes, 'should anything go wrong during that meeting, I've already devised an escape plan.'

Theron laughed tearfully. 'I don't doubt it.' They pulled away from each other completely and Theron leaned against his headrest. He sighed loudly. 'We sound like a married couple.'

Conor chuckled as he leaned back in his seat. He took Theron's hand and interlaced their fingers.

'I won't ever stop loving you, Theron, I know that. I tried and failed miserably at it.'

'Same.' Theron smiled fondly. 'I was in love with you even before I knew what romance was. I just . . . have always loved you.' He turned his head to Conor, who turned his head to him. 'We *should* get married.'

Conor grinned, bringing Theron's hand to his lips, and kissed it. 'I've wanted that since we were kids.'

'When you told me that on the roof, I don't know, it felt like a relief. That's how I know this feels right.'

'Funny how none of this feels like we're moving too fast.'

'It feels too slow.'

'That's because nothing can change how we feel about each other.' Conor placed the palm of Theron's hand on his face. 'We spent our lives together before, devoted to each other. Now we just get to do it as proper lovers.' Conor and Theron beamed at each other. Then Conor turned back to face the front. 'So what's the plan, detective?'

'We speak with Martha, sort out the current . . . situation, and then take it from there.'

'And never leave each other's side.'

Conor's smile sent warmth to Theron's heart.

* * *

Conor fidgeted nervously beside Theron as Martha glanced up, brows raised.

Theron and Conor sat in the chairs in front of her desk. Martha was a stern-looking woman with a strong build, and Theron knew that just sitting in the office Conor had broken into a mere month and a half ago had the thief suffering from nervous shakes.

'What's this about, Theron? Who's your friend?'

Conor leaned towards Theron and muttered under his breath. 'You didn't tell her who I am?'

Theron grimaced. 'This is Conor.'

Martha nodded once. 'You a detective?'

'I'm . . .' Conor took a deep breath. Theron reached for his hand and interlaced their fingers, wanting to convey confidence. 'I'm Vulpis.'

Martha arched her brows as her eyes widened. She pointed from Theron to Conor and back again. 'I take it this means you two have figured things out?'

Theron was puzzled. '*That's* your first question?'

Martha shrugged, turning her attention to Conor. 'Ever since he joined this firm, he has not shut up about you. Not once.'

'Wait,' began Conor, turning his head to Theron, 'you told her about me? As in that Vulpis was the best friend that moved away?'

'Yeah?' Theron grimaced again. He produced the printed documents from his briefcase and placed them on Martha's desk. 'I found a clause that stipulates the conditions for surveyed probation and I believe Conor fits the criteria.'

Martha took the papers, glancing so quickly before placing them on her desk, face-down. She steepled her fingers. 'I'm going to have to make some calls, and Conor has the right to an attorney. If we do this, you're both going to have to sign some documents.'

Conor nodded. 'I'm willing to be more . . . legal.'

Martha let out a small laugh. 'Good to know. Maybe this one,' she gave Theron a pointed stare, 'can stop pining.' She paused. 'For real, though, I'm happy for you both. Honestly.' She sobered. 'Listen, I'm going to have to pull some strings, but I've been doing my own research and I think I know what else can work. If all goes well, Vulpis can keep doing what he does best, retrieve stolen items for people, but it will have to be as a detective for this agency.'

'I can work with that,' said Conor. His careful reply had Theron's heart soaring with hope.

'This also means . . .' Again, Martha steepled her fingers. 'You're our Vulpis expert, Theron, so Conor will be under your scrutiny.'

Theron perked up, his heart thumping with excitement. 'You mean, like, my partner?'

'That is the definition of two people who work cases and missions together, yes,' Martha confirmed, her tone unfazed.

'Thank you so much!'

'Don't thank me yet. Oh, and Vulpis – Conor – you'll have to sign with your full legal name.'

'Gotcha.'

Martha glanced at their clasped hands. 'You've really gone and figured it out, eh?'

'I wouldn't say we've figured *everything* out,' admitted Theron. 'But we've committed.'

'Aw.' Martha looked suddenly giddy for them and it made Theron's face feel hot. Conor blushed. Then she was all-business again and shooing them out with a quick wave of her hand.

'I've got work to do. We meet in two days.'

'That's perfect, I have one last job I need to do before signing into the legal route,' said Conor.

Martha pointed a finger at him. 'Don't get caught.'

Conor blushed. 'My hunter caught me a long time ago.'

The two men stood, hands still clasped and stepped out of Martha's office and outside. Conor grinned at Theron bringing Theron's hand close to his heart – it still thudded fast but he looked relieved and was no longer shaking like when they'd entered Martha's office. Conor lowered his face, bringing Theron's hand up and kissing it. Then he placed something cold in it.

'Food for Fidelis is behind the pantry. Don't wait up, I'll be gone a few.' Conor leaned in for a quick peck on the lips that was so fast Theron barely registered it. 'Love you.'

Conor jumped up to grab a railing and propelled himself with a kick like an acrobat. Theron gaped, surprised and unable to call Conor's name.

He looked down at the item in his hand. Keys. He exhaled as he grinned. Conor had given him the keys to his place.

With a bounce in his step, Theron walked to the car and drove to Conor's penthouse apartment. He hesitated as he entered. 'Uh, Fidelis?'

The dog barked happily and strutted towards him. She smelled his feet.

'Remember me?'

In response, Fidelis sat on Theron's foot.

'I'll take that as a yes.'

He scratched the dog's head before entering the penthouse proper. He took the time to relax, play with the dog, and snoop around a bit. He messaged Conor. *I miss you.* And then realised that was useless when he heard Conor's phone buzz right after hitting send.

'Right. Conor doesn't bring his phone with him on a job.'

That night Theron slept in Conor's bed, snuggling to the pillows that smelt like Conor. Fidelis slept at his feet. She seemed to acclimatise to him quickly. Theron took that as a good sign.

Theron passed by his place to pack a few items. He began a list. He didn't want to spring it on Conor – moving in – but he was mentally getting ready for it.

Theron began to worry when Conor didn't return on the second night. His heart was tight and his constant fear of losing Conor, that Conor would leave him, lingered.

Theron snooped some more, hoping to find a clue that would reassure him, a note Conor might have left behind for him.

He found a piece of stationery turned over beneath some papers. Theron took it. His heart sank when he read the words on the paper.

I'm sorry, it began. *I tried to understand where you were coming from. I tried to help you see my perspective. But I realise now that we're just too different from each other, we'll never see eye to eye on this. I can't be something I'm not. And I can't not be who I truly am. I hope someday you'll come to accept that. You'll always be in my heart. But for now, this has to be goodbye. I need some time apart. I hope you understand.*

'No,' whispered Theron.

He clamped a hand on his mouth as tears spilled from his eyes. His heart felt like it was being ripped open.

'Conor,' he wept.

He felt like an idiot, to believe Conor had chosen him and would never leave him now that they had declared their love for each other. His mind whirled, not knowing if Conor had tried and changed his mind or if he had lied to him.

Theron clutched the letter, holding it close to his heart, feeling like he couldn't breathe as he heaved.

He backed away and lay in bed, wrapping his arms around Conor's pillow and burying his face in it, trying to smell Conor's smell and imbibe it permanently.

He cried himself to sleep.

CHAPTER 9

When Theron awoke, someone was stroking the back of their fingers on his cheek.

Theron opened his eyes and gasped at the sight of Conor lying in bed, an arm wrapped around him, his expression one of concern.

'Conor?' Theron quavered.

'Your face is streaked. Have you been crying? Babe, what's wrong?'

'I thought . . .' Theron began to weep anew. 'I thought you left me.'

'Theron, I could never – not ever.' Conor shook his head. 'That first time, it wasn't by choice and I will never choose that. I promised you to stay by your side and to commit to you. I'm serious about us. You're the love of my life.' He pressed his lips together, bringing Theron into his embrace. 'Is this because I was gone an extra day?'

Theron pulled back and lifted the paper from beneath the pillow, now scrunched.

Conor's eyes widened as he took it from Theron. 'Yeah, I can see how you might misinterpret this.' His brows creased in apology and he cupped Theron's face. 'Aw babe, this letter, I wrote it for my parents.'

Theron's heart skipped a beat. He felt like an idiot – again.

'Yeah, they . . . They don't exactly approve of my sexuality. My relationship with them has been strained at best.'

'Oh god, Conor, I'm so sorry. And here I was thinking the worst.'

Conor placed the letter aside. 'I get it. I left once, and didn't protest when it happened. You fear me abandoning you. Just as I fear you hating me out of the blue. That's why I've been trying to be the perfect boyfriend . . . fiancé? I don't know, I'm just trying to be perfect for you.'

'You are!' declared Theron.

Conor flipped Theron onto his back, clasping both of his hands and holding them to the sides of his head as he loomed above him, their bodies pressed intimately together.

'Theron, I promise, I am never leaving you. I am with you and committed to this – to us – for good.' Tears sparkled in Conor's eyes. 'I'm so sorry I ever hurt you to cause you such sorrow today.'

'I'm sorry I ever hurt you too.'

Conor offered Theron a tender smile. 'I picked something up on my way back. That's why it took longer. I had them custom-made.' Conor produced a small box and opened it to reveal two rings.

Theron's eyes widened. 'Did you steal this?'

Conor shook his head. 'Standard job, retrieve a box of photos buried in a childhood home garden. But this? I stopped on my way there and back.'

Conor took the rings out. Each had a different engraved design, both were silver. 'A fox – mine.'

'And a bow with a pulled arrow,' said Theron.

'A hunter.'

'A thief and his hunter,' whispered Theron.

Conor took Theron's left hand and slipped the ring on his ring finger. Theron heaved with emotion. Conor whispered. 'Put the other one on me.'

Theron obliged. Then they interlaced their hands once more.

'I love you, my hunter.'

Theron let out a small tear-filled laugh, and whispered. 'I love you, my thief.'

Their lips met in a fervent kiss as they wept more declarations. And they continued to kiss long after they had made love.

* * *

Conor's heart was thudding so fast, he was so nervous. This was a commitment he never thought he'd make, but he was doing it – for Theron. A judge had signed, the attorney had signed, Martha and Theron had signed. And now Conor was signing.

This didn't just commit Conor to Theron, but to the law, to respecting certain conditions and rules, and to being checked in on every day. To full-on probation. He was lucky he could do this instead of jail time.

After they had met with Martha, they had met with a few others and gone through the boring bits of ensuring Conor's probation would be approved.

The pen slipped in Conor's sweat-filled fingers. He steadied it. And then . . . He did it. He signed. He placed the pen down on top of the contract.

Martha held out her hand to Conor. 'Welcome to the firm, Detective Vulpis.'

Beaming, Theron turned to Conor and interlaced their hands. 'Welcome, partner.'

Conor bit his lower lip, grinning from ear to ear.

* * *

Several weeks later.

'I'll race you to our destination!' Conor announced excitedly, as he and Theron grabbed their jackets.

'You do realise I'll be in a vehicle?'

'There are no traffic lights up on the roofs,' argued Conor.

Theron rolled his eyes. 'Don't be reckless, darling.'

'Less banter, more focus, gentlemen,' Martha's voice crackled over their earpieces. 'I don't care how either of you get there. I care that you get there on time.'

Blushing, the two men chuckled.

'This might not be your first mission but it's no reason to start slacking.'

'Yes, ma'am,' they both replied.

Petting Fidelis goodbye, the two lovers stepped out of the apartment. Conor bounded up in the setting sun to the roof as Theron headed down to the parking lot.

As he drove, Theron glanced up every chance he got. Conor was taking the same streets, for the most part, and Theron glimpsed him leaping from roof to roof and scaling down emergency stairs.

As Theron parked the car in front of the museum, Conor landed in front of the car, hands on his hips. Theron clicked his tongue and chuckled, shaking his head.

Theron stepped out of the car, and Conor announced, 'A whole five seconds earlier than you.'

Theron suppressed his smile, stuffing his hands in his pockets. That's when he found a note.

'When did you slip this in, darling?'

Conor shrugged.

Happy anniversary.

Theron rubbed his forehead. 'Which anniversary?' He shrugged as he asked it. He looked up at Conor. 'Do we count from the moment we declared our love for each other after finding each other again? Or when we kissed and made love for the first time? Became partners? When I moved in with you? Or maybe the day we decided to spend the rest of our lives together? Which was the day after we made love for the first time.'

Conor shrugged, fiddling with the ring on his finger. Theron fiddled with *his* in response.

'We'll figure that out after, lest Martha scolds us,' suggested Conor.

'Thank you, gentlemen.'

Theron could hear the suppressed smile in Martha's tone, and it made him chuckle.

Theron and Conor stepped up to the museum's door. Conor scowled and pointed at the knob.

'Is this supposed to be left open like this?'

Theron's heart leapt to his throat and he pulled out his pistol, levelling it as he stepped protectively in front of Conor.

'Get behind me.'

Theron led the way, gun raised, checking every direction as he slowly entered the museum. It was quiet.

They had been expected. They had a warrant. They were here to negotiate after closing hours.

While some jobs required actual thieving – legal thieving – this one required more security measures.

Conor had tracked down the item, and then Theron and Martha had done the work to make the exchange legal.

However, *this* was not normal. It was dark and still.

With Conor breathing noiselessly behind him, Theron continued forward, his shoes barely making a sound, and up the stairs to the second floor. He dared not call out, in case that would alert the intruder of their presence.

Theron arrived at the glass casing where the quarry should have been sitting. It was empty. As Conor joined his side, Theron's eyes landed on the bloody scene at his feet.

'Oh god,' he whispered.

Conor yelped and clamped a hand to his mouth, turning away from the scene – he had never seen a dead body before.

Theron wrapped an arm around Conor in a protective embrace, bringing his face to his chest, and placed his free hand on his head, stroking his hair.

'It's okay. I'm here.'

Theron swallowed hard. He turned his face away from the scene as well.

'What's going on in there, boys?' Martha's voice came over the earpiece.

'We have a situation,' said Theron, his voice low and rough, his breath shaking.

'What kind of situation?' demanded Martha.

'Someone's taken the item and . . .' Theron exhaled through his nose, 'and replaced it with a body.'

His hold on Conor tightened and he clenched his jaw. 'Someone's trying to frame Vulpis for murder.'

To be continued.

<u>THANK YOU SO MUCH FOR READING</u>

If you enjoyed this story,
please consider taking a few moments
to write a review on Amazon or Goodreads.
It would mean so much.

Thank you.

ALSO BY

Also Written by Eidahs

Sanguine Sincerity
(https://binkyproductions.com/supernaturalromance)

Like Father, Not Like Sons
Legacy Takedown
Of Sullied Dreams and Beaten Hearts
Butchery At the Debauchery
(www.binkyproductions.com/shortstories)

Also Published by Binky Ink

Stardust Destinies I: Variate Facing
Stardust Destinies II: The Drought
(https://binkyproductions.com/stardustdestinies)

The Hidden Cove: Pirate's Misadventure
(www.binkyproductions.com/shortstories)

Eidahs is a pseudonym for all mature written works, from thrillers to erotic romance. Eidahs in pronunciation sounds elven in nature, which is why she chose it, to tap into her love of fantasy, a genre that couples well with super-natural and preternatural, dark fantasy, and romance.

Eidahs is also the nickname 'Shadie' backwards, repre-senting the shadow self, innermost desires, and a spectrum of emotions, most notably, passion, sorrow, rage, and delight, which Eidahs loves to incorporate in her writing. Enticing readers and evoking the characters' emotions when she writes has guided her inspiration to spell many short stories on Medium and a series of books under this pen name.

Connect with Binky Ink:

WordPress Website & Blog
        https://binkyproductions.com/binkyinkwriting
Medium – Main Profile
        https://medium.com/@BinkyInkWriting
X (Twitter) https://twitter.com/binkyinkwriting